Be More
Bernard

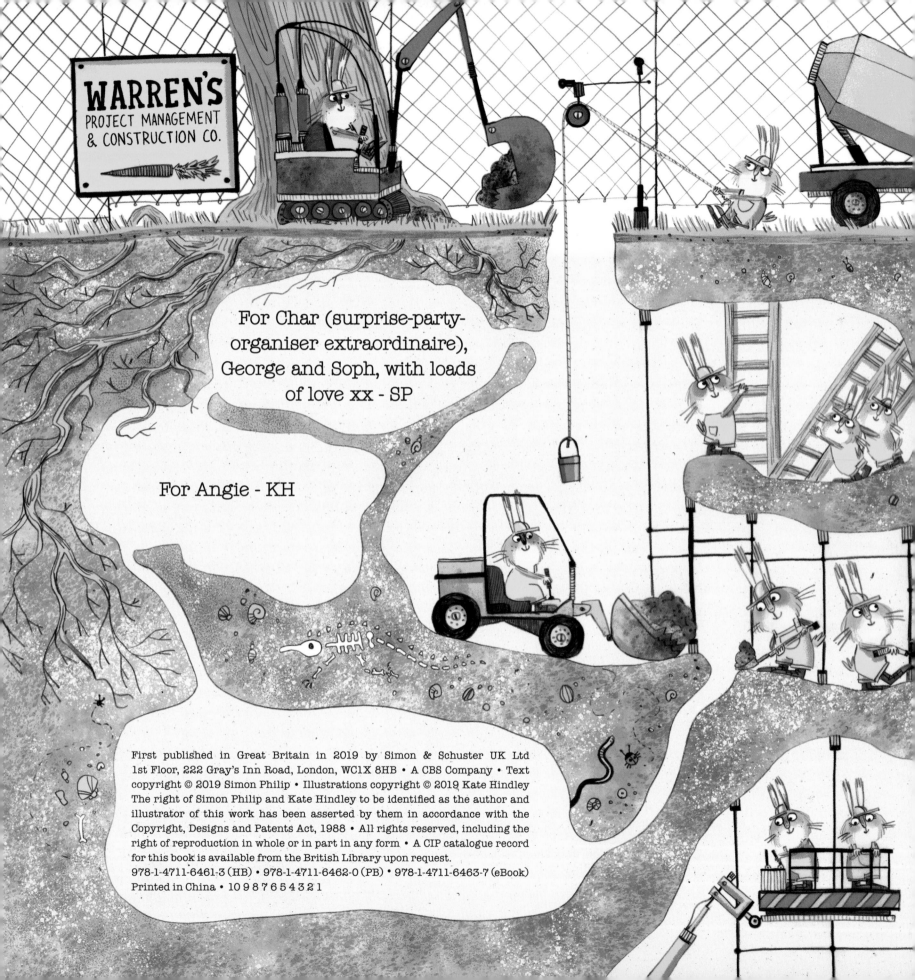

WARREN'S
PROJECT MANAGEMENT
& CONSTRUCTION CO.

For Char (surprise-party-
organiser extraordinaire),
George and Soph, with loads
of love xx - SP

For Angie - KH

First published in Great Britain in 2019 by Simon & Schuster UK Ltd
1st Floor, 222 Gray's Inn Road, London, WC1X 8HB • A CBS Company • Text
copyright © 2019 Simon Philip • Illustrations copyright © 2019 Kate Hindley
The right of Simon Philip and Kate Hindley to be identified as the author and
illustrator of this work has been asserted by them in accordance with the
Copyright, Designs and Patents Act, 1988 • All rights reserved, including the
right of reproduction in whole or in part in any form • A CIP catalogue record
for this book is available from the British Library upon request.
978-1-4711-6461-3 (HB) • 978-1-4711-6462-0 (PB) • 978-1-4711-6463-7 (eBook)
Printed in China • 10 9 8 7 6 5 4 3 2 1

RABBITS
AT WORK

Be More
Bernard

Simon Philip
& Kate Hindley

SIMON & SCHUSTER
London   New York   Sydney   Toronto   New Delhi

I acted like a bunny should act.
I did what I believed was right.

I twitched my nose.

I pricked my ears.

I grazed on grass and dug
deep holes in gardens and fields,
because that's what bunnies do.

And when I wasn't
doing those things,
I tried to look as cute
as I possibly could.

When the other bunnies bounced,

I bounced.

When they hopped,

I hopped.

When they slept, I did too.
Like them, I dreamed.

But MY dreams
weren't the same.

They were less . . . rabbity.

More . . . unusual.

I tried to pretend that all was normal,
that my dreams didn't matter.

"Bernard," they'd ask, **"what do you dream about?"**

"The same as you," I'd lie.

"Carrots?" they'd ask.
"Yes," I'd lie again.
"The orange ones."

They were terrible, TERRIBLE lies.

Day after day, I continued my act,
being the same as everyone else.
Twitching.
Digging.
Looking as cute as
I possibly could.

I ate more lettuce than
any bunny should ever
have to eat.

BRIAN'S FABULOUS

~B. BUNNY G AUGHTE

BREKKIE BAPS

TODAY'S
SPECIAL:
POO
BAPS

GGIES CO

The rest of them ate other things, too.
Things that shouldn't be eaten!
And that's where I drew the line.

I CAN'T DO THIS ANY MORE, I decided.

I started small.

At first, it felt a little odd,
bouncing when the others hopped.

Hopping when the others bounced.

But soon, it felt strangely normal.

At work, I acted just like before.

Well, mostly.

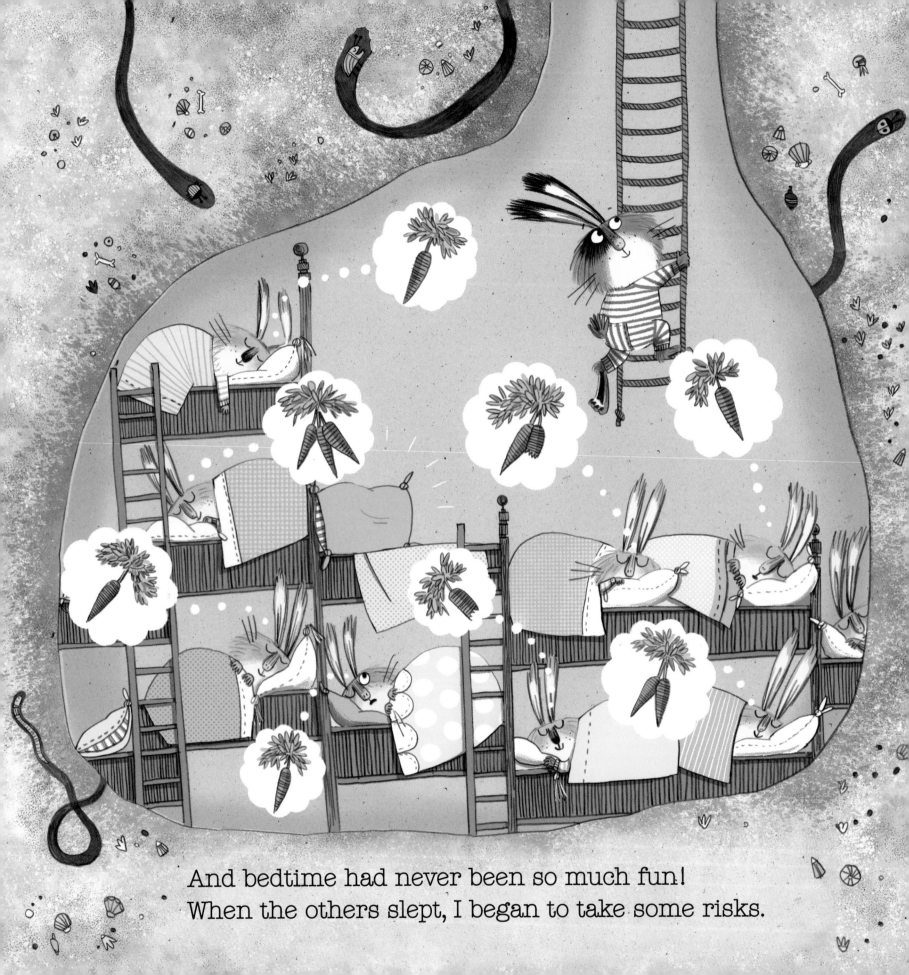

And bedtime had never been so much fun!
When the others slept, I began to take some risks.

A few bunnies were suspicious,
but most didn't take much notice.

BERTIE & BRENDA'S

Then, when the moment felt right
(at Bertie and Brenda's Annual Bunny Ball),
I finally went further –

and notice they most definitely did.

TUESDAYS

BUNNY
BASKET
BALL

LOST
PANTS!

BUNNY BALL

They stood startled, like . . .

well . . .

rabbits caught in the headlights.

"You can't wear that!" they cried.

"You're a bunny!" they insisted.

"We're all the same!" they chorused.

But **I** wasn't!

I twirled and sashayed away from their shouts, until my world was spinning faster than it had EVER spun before.

I felt free! And fabulous! And me!

(And, well, a bit sick.
Probably because of the lettuce.
And maybe the spinning, too.)

I didn't just bounce and hop.

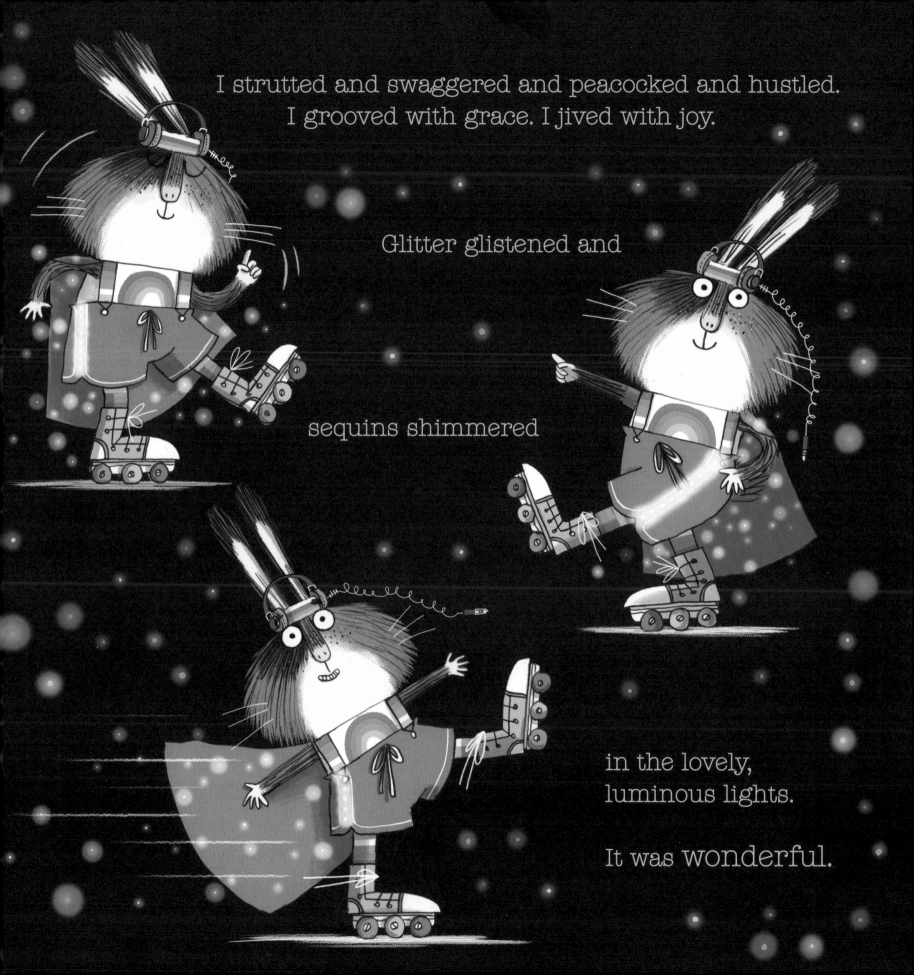

I strutted and swaggered and peacocked and hustled.
I grooved with grace. I jived with joy.

Glitter glistened and

sequins shimmered

in the lovely,
luminous lights.

It was WONDERFUL.

Most of the others were horrified,
blinded by the twinkle of my toes.
And maybe the disco ball.
Possibly my outfit, too.

"He stands out like a bunny at a disco!" Brian cried.

"He IS a bunny at a disco!" Bonnie squealed.

"Doesn't he know we're supposed to be the SAME?" Bella wailed.

But there was one bunny, Betsy, who wasn't horrified.

"I . . . like it," she said. "It's . . . different."

Soon, Betsy was just
as groovy

and happy

and different

. . . as me.

It got the others thinking.

And, before I knew it . . .

... we were all as different as each other!

Once we were all boogied out,
we sat in happy silence.
Then I asked the question I was desperate
for them to answer.

"Do you really dream of carrots?" I said.

For a while, nobody said a word.
But eventually, Brian spoke.

"I hate carrots," he said.

"I dream of cheese."

"Me too," Bonnie smiled, "and music!"

"It's ballet for me," Betsy explained.

"And I dream of hats!" Bella laughed.

"Fabulous, fancy hats."

As they shared their dreams,
I could tell their hearts were dancing just like mine.

RABBITS AT WORK

And so now, even though we're all the same in many ways, we can all agree that . . .

. . . being yourself

is the BEST thing a bunny can be!